To Michalis,
who first showed me the constellations
through a huge telescope.
A.P.

To my niece, Stella Griva,
who has all the constellations of the sky
in her hair and eyes.
V.G.

TALES FROM THE GREEK MYTHS

Callisto and the Book of the Sky

Antonis Papatheodoulou
Illustrated by Vassilis Grivas

Translated by Joshua Barley

μεταιχμιο ◑

1st edition April 2018

ORIGINAL TITLE Αντώνης Παπαθεοδούλου,
Η Καλλιστώ και το βιβλίο του ουρανού, Μεταίχμιο 2017

TRANSLATED FROM THE GREEK LANGUAGE BY Joshua Barley
ILLUSTRATED BY Vassilis Grivas

ISBN 978-618-03-1454-0
AUXIL. COMPU. CODE 81454
C.E.P. 4337 C.P. 9747

ISO 9001

No 110
EN 45012
Accredited

QMSCERT No 04/1230/279
QMSCERT No 04/1230/279.1

Bookstores
1. 18 ASKLIPIOU STR., 106 80 ATHENS
TEL. +30 210 3647433, FAX: +30 211 3003562
Internet Site: www.metaixmio.gr
e-mail: metaixmio@metaixmio.gr

2. POLYCHOROS, 118 IPPOKRATOUS STR., 114 72 ATHENS
TEL. +30 210 3003580, FAX: +30 211 3003581

'Do you want to read a story?'

'I didn't bring one with me, daddy. I left them all at home.'

'We'll find something. Come on...'

'We're going to find a story in the forest?'

'Absolutely! The glades in the forest are full of stories.

'OK, let's go. But let me get my torch from the tent. It's night and there's no moon. How will we read without any light?'

'No! Don't get the torch. The story we are looking for doesn't need light. To be precise, the less light there is, the clearer it will be.'

'I have no idea what you're talking about.'

'Well, sit here on this tree trunk and look upwards. What do you see?'

'The stars in the sky...'

'Are you sure? I see an open book, with stories! Look carefully at the stars, do you see the shape they make?'

'Yes, they look like a wagon.'

'Yes, and like anything else?'
'And like a saucepan...'

Look more carefully at the stars, not only at the bright ones but also at those that don't shine so much...

It is the body of a bear. And that is the name of the constellation, the Great Bear.'

'And what is a bear doing in the sky?'

'It's a long story. It begins many, many years ago in the Peloponnese, in Arcadia, where the mythical king Lycaon was ruling. His daughter, Callisto, was very beautiful. Everyone was dazzled by her beauty and everyone wanted to marry her. Callisto, however, had sworn an oath to always follow Artemis, the goddess of hunting. She went around the mountains and forests with her, hunting game.

'Until one day, when Zeus, king of the gods, saw her from high up on his throne on Olympus. He could not resist her beauty. He came down from Olympus, made her his wife and had a child with her: Arcas. That is where Arcadia takes its name from.

'The goddess Hera, however, who never left Zeus' infidelity unpunished, flew into a rage. And in order to destroy forever the beauty of this nymph, who had even made Zeus fall in love with her, she transformed her... into a bear!

'Callisto hid in fear in the forest. Her famous beauty had been lost forever, and the nymph, who for so many years had been the goddess Artemis' best co-hunter, had now become the hunted.

Maia, one of the Pleiades (the Seven Sisters) raised her son Arcas, and when he grew up he became as good a hunter as his mother. He was brave and an excellent marksman. When he drew his bow, nothing could escape him.

'One day Callisto saw her son hunting in the forest. She so longed to be near him and admire him that she forgot that she had been transformed into a bear.

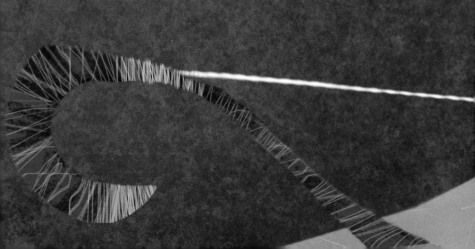

'When Arcas saw the bear approaching, he drew his bow and aimed at it. Zeus, watching from above on Olympus, could not allow something terrible to happen – to let Arcas shoot his own mother without re-alising it. Before he managed to shoot the arrow from his bow, he transformed Arcas into a little bear. And to save both of them from the anger of Hera, who was always planning some new punishment, he raised them up high into the heavens and trans-formed them into constellations.'

'And where is Callisto's little bear?'

'Look opposite the Great Bear. Do you see a smaller shape that looks just like her?'

'Yes! There it is!'

'That is the Little Bear. Mother and son have lived up there since then. Do you see how we found a story to read tonight? One with words and images. And without any light, because this story shines on its own.

'We have other pages too. We can read a story every night: the story of the hunter Orion and the Scorpion that Artemis sent to bite him. They were both transformed into stars in the sky. Or of how the Seven Sisters were transformed into stars, or Perseus and Andromeda and her parents Kassiope and Kifeas, and even the god Apollo's Lyre, made by Hermes: all of these stories and many more are written on the pages of the sky.'

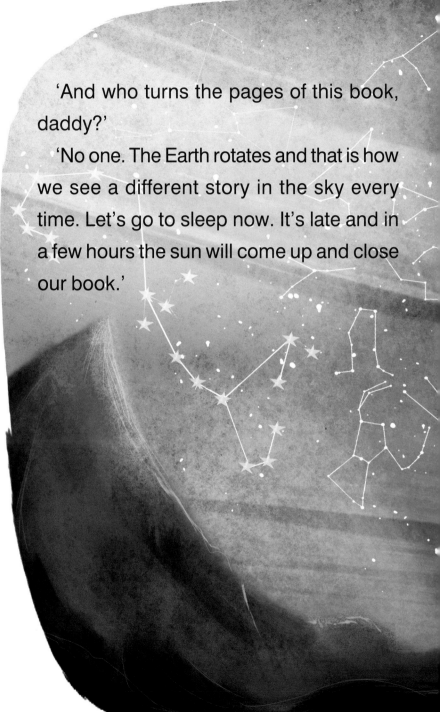

'And who turns the pages of this book, daddy?'

'No one. The Earth rotates and that is how we see a different story in the sky every time. Let's go to sleep now. It's late and in a few hours the sun will come up and close our book.'

'Daddy, do you know why the ancient people transformed the night sky into a whole book of myths and stories?'

'Why do you think?'

'So they could be sure.'

'Sure about what?'

'Sure that all of the children of the world could have at least one book of their own.'

PLAYING
WITH THE
MYTH

Educational
material
by Maria Gonidaki

THE MYTH OF CALLISTO

Humans have been looking at the sky and the stars since long ago. They saw that some groups of stars – constellations – formed the shapes of animals or objects. Therefore, their imagination started making up stories and connecting them with existing myths.

The myth of Callisto was made in this way:

Callisto was the daughter of the king of Arcadia, Lycaon.

She lived in the mountains of Arcadia and hunted with the other nymphs who served the goddess Artemis. When Zeus saw her, he fell in love and had a son with her, Arcas. When Hera found out, she was very angry and decided to punish Callisto: she transformed her into a bear. According to another version of the myth, Zeus transformed Callisto into a bear to avoid the wrath of Hera. Hermes took Arcas, Callisto's son, following Zeus' command, and gave him to his mother, Maia, to raise.

When Arcas grew up, he became a good hunter and went hunting in the mountains of Arcadia. One day, Callisto, transformed into a bear, saw him and recognised him (even though she had the form of a bear, she still had a human mind). From her longing to see him, she approached him without realising the danger. When he was about to shoot his arrow, Zeus pitied them and transformed Arcas into a little bear. Then, so they would avoid Hera's anger, he made them into constellations and helped them be together forever. Callisto shines in the night sky as the Great Bear, and Arcas as the Little Bear!

THINK ABOUT THIS...

The myth of Callisto is one of the few cases we have of a double transformation: Callisto was first transformed into a bear and then into a constellation.

CROSSWORD

1. The father of Callisto.
2. The Great Bear is a...
3. The goddess of hunting.
4. Who transformed Callisto into a bear?
5. The father of Arcas.
6. This nymph raised Arcas.

▶ Look at the painting below from an ancient Greek vase.

- Who could the figures be?
- Which feature helps you recognise which male figure it is?

▶ Match up the constellations

(Look up on the internet about the myth that is connected to each constellation).

PERSEUS

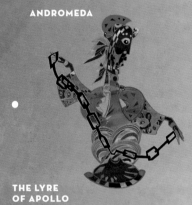

ANDROMEDA

THE LYRE OF APOLLO

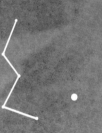

CASSIOPEIA

▶ Find these well-known constellations in the word search.

ORION, CEPHEUS, SCORPIUS, PEGASUS, CENTAURUS, CYGNUS

K	A	L	L	C	R	P	A	H	I	A	T
B	K	A	L	E	I	E	P	R	E	I	A
K	M	M	P	N	X	S	E	E	L	H	W
A	W	K	A	T	L	Y	G	T	I	K	O
L	Z	O	J	A	L	Y	A	M	R	L	C
H	Γ	K	A	U	L	I	S	T	E	I	E
I	S	C	O	R	P	I	U	S	P	P	P
O	S	X	R	U	J	N	S	I	Ω	G	H
V	Z	O	W	S	A	L	H	O	N	H	E
H	Z	B	M	A	T	S	T	O	M	N	U
C	Y	G	N	U	S	H	N	E	I	Λ	S
K	A	L	L	I	R	O	R	I	O	N	X

- ▶ The bear is one of the favourite animals of Greek mythology and of the folk tradition. In the15th century, the brown bear lived in the whole of Europe. Now it lives in small, isolated populations and is in danger of extinction. The basic reasons why the population is declining are: **a.** Hunting. **b.** The continuous destruction of the bears' natural habitat.

- Over the last years, thanks to the decisions of the European Union and the efforts of environmental organisations, it seems that the situation could change: the population of the brown bear in Europe has increased 7% in 7 years, from 15,800 in 2005 to 17,000 in 2012, while in various regions, the rate of change is very high. In Karelia (in Russia), for example, the population has doubled from 850 to 1,700 and in Scandinavia it has increased from 2,600 to 3,400 (in 1930 there were only 130 bears in Scandinavia). In the Cantabrian Mountains of Spain, the population has doubled over the last decade, from 100 to 200.

- Visit the websites of the environmental organisations below and see how you can help protect the environment, particularly in preserving this wonderful animal.

www.worldwildlife.org/species/brown-bear

www.euronatur.org/en/what-we-do/endangered-species/bear/bears-in-europe/

www.fondationsegre.org/urgent-measures-for-the-conservation-of-the-critically-endangered-marsican-brown-bear-in-central-apennines/

Vassilis Grivas was born in Lamia. He has worked with many publishing houses as an illustrator of children's books and has illustrated more than 100 books and dust-jackets in Greece and abroad (America, China, Great Britain, Italy). He is also a painter, having taken part in group exhibitions as well as two solo exhibitions.

In 2006 he wrote and illustrated a fairytale inspired by the folk tradition, *Konstantis and the Dazzling Girl*. In 2014, his fairytale *Zaf the Persian Cat* was published in the USA by Tate Publishing and Enterprises.

Vassilis Grivas

Antonis Papatheodoulou

Antonis Papatheodoulou has published more than 40 books for children in Greece. Books of his have been transformed into theatre and puppet theatre plays and have been translated to French, Portuguese, Spanish, Galician, Catalan, Basque, Japanese, Chinese & Korean. His book *One last letter* (illustrated by I. Samartzi) won the International Compostela Prize for picture books 2016. His book *The city that drove out war* (illustrated by M. Delivoria) won the Greek State Picturebook Book Award for 2011 and the 2011 Illustrated Children's Book Award of *Diavazo* magazine. His book *The good and the bad Pirates* (illustrated by I. Samartzi) won the Greek State Picturebook Book Award for 2012 and the Illustrated Book Award of the Greek section of IBBY for 2012. The book *Boats that sailed Imagination* that he co-wrote with M. Angelidou won the Non Fiction Award of the Greek section of IBBY for 2015. Five of his books have been included in the White Ravens list of the International Children's Library of Munich.

TALES FROM THE GREEK MYTHS
SERIES

Maria Angelidou

The Cattle of Geryon

Illustrated by Iris Samartzi

TALES FROM THE GREEK MYTHS

Maria Angelidou

The Apples of the Hesperides

Illustrated by Iris Samartzi

TALES FROM THE GREEK MYTHS

Maria Angelidou

The Girdle of Hippolyta

Illustrated by Iris Samartzi

TALES FROM THE GREEK MYTHS

Maria Angelidou

The Capture of Cerberus

Illustrated by Iris Samartzi

TALES FROM THE GREEK MYTHS

Maria Angelidou

The Lernaean Hydra

Illustrated by Iris Samartzi

TALES FROM THE GREEK MYTHS

Maria Angelidou

The Stables of Augeas

Illustrated by Iris Samartzi

TALES FROM THE GREEK MYTHS

Kostas Poulos

The Riddle of the Sphinx

Illustrated by Sofia Papadopoulou

TALES FROM THE GREEK MYTHS

Kostas Poulos

The Song of the Sirens

Illustrated by Sofia Papadopoulou

TALES FROM THE GREEK MYTHS